$18.45

Stop
Kiss

Stop
Kiss

BY
D I A N A   S O N

THE OVERLOOK PRESS
WOODSTOCK & NEW YORK

First published in the United States in 1999 by
The Overlook Press, Peter Mayer Publishers, Inc.
Lewis Hollow Road
Woodstock, New York 12498
Web: http://www.overlookpress.com

Copyright © 1999 by Diana Son

Library of Congress Cataloging-in-Publication Data

Son, Diana.
Stop kiss / Diana Son.
p.   cm.
1. Young women—Crimes against—New York (State)—New York
Drama.   2. Hate crimes—New York (State)—New York Drama.
3. Homophobia—New York (State)—New York Drama.   I. Title.

Book design and type formatting by Bernard Schleifer
Manufactured in the United States of America
First Edition
1 3 5 7 9 8 6 4 2
ISBN 0-87951-737-9

for Mom, Dad,
and Michael

Thank you Tim Sandford at Playwrights Horizons and Paul Lister at Amblin-Dreamworks for commissioning the play. Cheers to Chay Yew and the Asian Theatre Workshop at the Mark Taper Forum; and Elissa Adams and the Playwrights Center for their reading and workshop opportunities.

A final sweep of gratitude to: Heather Mazur, Angel Desai, Liam Craig, Matt Shepherd, Kara Hrabosky, Rafi Levavy, Debbie Fowlkes, Holly Simmons, Fritz Masten, Natalie Norris, Chuck Dorman, Wade Raley, Lisa Peterson, David Greenspan, Todd London and New Dramatists, Donna Brodie and the Writer's Room, Morgan Jenness, Martha Fedorko, Nancy Weber, and Arnold Dolin.

A special place of thanks for Sarah Jane Leigh, first my friend, now my agent. My hero.

ACKNOWLEDGMENTS

For her trust, graciousness and commitment, I thank Jessica Hecht. Her involvement from the first reading on made my job of writing unusually fun. I'm also grateful to Jo Bonney for reading every draft and half-draft with long curls of faxed pages in between. A meeting with Jo seemed more like an exciting conversation than a rigorous dramaturgical commission, which in fact it was. Good trick, Jo. My happy thanks to the cast of the premiere production: Sandra Oh for her effortless courage and vivacity; Kevin Carroll for his elegance and dedication, Rick Holmes for his inventiveness and compassion; Saul Stein for his dignity. Saundra McClain for her wisdom; Brooke Smith for stepping in, stepping up, and knocking our socks off; and C.J. Wilson for his huge heart. Designers Narelle Sissons, Kaye Voyce, Jim Vermeulen, Shawn Gallagher, and David Van Tieghem did precise work with collaborative spirits; and we were all lead by Buzz Cohen—the legend is true.

I thank George Wolfe, who doubled as trusting producer and *deus ex machina*; Bonnie Metzgar, who gave us tireless care (I'm sure she sleeps standing up, smoking); Nick Schwartz-Hall, who shepherded us through the rough spots; Bill Coyle, who went beyond and then further; Merv Antonio and Shirley Fishman who were insightful and protective; and ultimate thanks to Shelby Jiggets-Tivony, who brought *Stop Kiss* to the Public Theater. I saw my first play ever at the Public Theater and it was a thrill to have *Stop Kiss* debut there.

INTRODUCTION

There are many reasons to celebrate *Stop Kiss* by Diana Son: Its craftsmanship is exhilarating. It's deeply appealing and effortlessly funny. It brilliantly captures how we all craft language to conceal and protect ourselves—and how our seemingly inarticulate, incomplete thoughts and awkward silences can, in fact, truly reveal our deepest longings. *Stop Kiss* shows us something about the process of healing, the cowardice of guilt, and the bravery of committing to something outside of yourself. In our intensely polarized world, where isolation and indifference are legitimized under the banner of urban self-preservation, Diana Son is both an artist and a humanist. She deeply understands both the joy and the pain of vulnerability, and that the not-so-simple act of caring, shared between two people, truly is a brave and revolutionary act. And in this smart and surprising comedy, she makes us understand it, too.

—GEORGE C. WOLFE

Stop Kiss premiered at the Joseph Papp Public Theater/New York Shakespeare Festival in New York on December 6, 1998. It was produced by George C. Wolfe and directed by Jo Bonney, with the following cast:

Callie	Jessica Hecht
Sara	Sandra Oh
Detective Cole	Saul Stein
Mrs. Winsley	Saundra McClain
George	Kevin Carroll
Peter	Rick Holmes
Nurse	Saundra McClain

Scenic Design was by Narelle Sissons, Costume Design by Kaye Voyce, Lighting Design by James Vermeulen, and Sound Design by David Van Tieghem.

Stop Kiss was written with support from Playwrights Horizons made possible in part by funds granted to the author through a program sponsored by Amblin Entertainment.

Callie, *late 20s to early 30s.*
Sara, *mid 20s to early 30s.*
George, *late 20s to early 30s.*
Peter, *mid 20s to early 30s.*
Mrs. Winsley, *late 30s to mid 40s.*
Detective Cole, *late 30s to mid 40s.*
Nurse, *late 30s to mid 40s. Can be doubled with Mrs. Winsley.*

Setting
New York City.

Time
Current.

Scene 1

Callie's apartment. Callie puts on a CD: The Emotions' "Best of My Love."

She ceremoniously closes all the blinds in her apartment, making sure each blade is turned over. She locks the front door and puts a piece of black tape over the peep hole.

As the vocals begin, Callie lip-syncs to the song with the polish of someone who has her own private karaoke often.

The phone rings. Callie turns off the CD like a busted teenager, and picks up the phone.

CALLIE

Hi George...yeah I know I'm late, I forgot this person is coming to my house at—
(Callie checks her watch)
—shit!...Well I would bring her along but I don't even know her. She's some friend of an old friend of someone I used to be frie—she just moved to New York and I said that I'd—I can't, what if she's some big dud and we all have a miserable time...Exactly, you'll all blame me. Give me half an hour, tops.

She sets the phone down. Her buzzer buzzes.

CALLIE

Yes?

SARA
(offstage, tentative)

It's Sara and—

CALLIE

Come on up!

Callie buzzes her in and looks at all the junk on her sofa; newspapers, several pairs of dirty socks, a box of kleenex, mail, a couple video-tapes, and a bra. She picks up the bra and heads for the bedroom.

The doorbell rings. Callie hides the bra and opens the door. Sara is holding a pet carrier.

CALLIE

Hi.

SARA

You're Callie.

CALLIE

Yes.

SARA

I'm Sara—
                    (She looks at the pet carrier)
This is Caesar and I can't believe you're doing this.

Callie gestures at the couch, notices it's a mess.

CALLIE

Please uh sit—

SARA

Some apartment.

CALLIE

I was cleaning.

SARA

It's huge—and the neighborhood—

Sara sits on a pile of books.

CALLIE

You can't be comfortable.

SARA

Oh I am.

14

CALLIE

Are you sure?

SARA

Very.

CALLIE

—Just...let me get rid of this stuff.

Callie gathers an armful of junk and heads toward her bedroom. As soon as she turns her back, Sara sits up and pulls out a large key ring full of sharp pointy keys and a candlestick from under her as she silently mouths "ow." She moves the objects to another part of the sofa, covers them with leftover junk—pulling out the keys so that they show—and makes a space for Callie. Callie re-enters.

CALLIE

Coffee!

SARA

—would be great.

SARA

Listen, this is so nice of you—

CALLIE

I was thinking about getting a cat anyway. Oh, my keys! This'll give me a chance to see if I can hack it.

SARA

That's how I feel about New York.

CALLIE
(*Sounds familiar*)

Oh yes.

Sara hops up and approaches Callie.

SARA

How long have you been here?

CALLIE

Eleven years.

SARA

I've lived in St. Louis my whole life. My parents live like, half an hour away. I go there for dinner when it's not even anybody's birthday. Things there—it's been, it is so—

CALLIE

Easy?

SARA

So easy.

CALLIE

It's hard here.

SARA

Good—*great*, I can't wait.

CALLIE

Yeah, you uh—what do you...do?

SARA

I teach. Third grade.

CALLIE

Well it won't be hard finding a job.

SARA

I already have one.

CALLIE

Where?

SARA

P.S. 32 in the Bronx.

CALLIE

What was the school like that you came from?

SARA

Society of Friends, a Quaker school.

Callie bursts into laughter.

CALLIE

I'm not—I'm not laughing at you, I'm laughing... *around*...

SARA

Its obviously—its *very*...but I can do good work there.

CALLIE

I'm sure you're a good teacher.

SARA

No you don't know, but I am.

Pause.

CALLIE

Where in the Bronx?

SARA

Tremont.

CALLIE

Is that where...Taft, is it Taft?

SARA

Taft High School?

CALLIE

You've heard of it?

SARA

Mm hm.

CALLIE

You know there was a guy who taught there, this rich white guy—

SARA

Yes I know.

Pause.

CALLIE

He got killed—

SARA

By a student. I'm here on a fellowship set up in his name.

CALLIE

How long is the fellowship?

SARA

Two years.

Callie offers Sara a coffee mug and raises hers in a toast.

CALLIE

Well, congratulations—

SARA

Thank you.

CALLIE

Best of luck—

Sara nods.

CALLIE

And...if it gets too rough—go home.

Callie touches her mug to Sara's, but Sara doesn't reciprocate.

SARA

What brought you to New York?

Callie inhales to prepare for her long and interesting answer then realizes she has none.

CALLIE

College.

SARA

And what keeps you?

CALLIE

Keeps me from what?

SARA

What do you *do*?

CALLIE

I...ruin things for everyone else.

SARA

You're Rudolph Giuliani?

CALLIE

I'm a traffic reporter for a twenty-four-hour news radio station.

SARA

(Impressed)

Helicopters!

CALLIE

"The inbound lane at the Holland Tunnel is closed due to a car accident. The Brooklyn-bound lane of the Williamsburg Bridge is under construction through 1999. The D train is not running due to a track fire. You can't get in. You can't get out. You can't get around. I'll be back in 10 minutes to tell you that nothing has changed."

SARA

Does that get to you?

Callie shrugs.

CALLIE

It's a living.

Sara checks out the apartment.

SARA

How long have you lived in this apartment?

CALLIE

Five years—well, two by myself—it's a funny—not haha—story.

SARA

It's o.k. (In other words, you don't have to tell me)

CALLIE

I moved in here with my boyfriend Tom. This was his aunt's apartment, she lived here for 20 years.

SARA

Your rent must be—

CALLIE

Lucky.

SARA

You are.

CALLIE

Well, I got the apartment, he got...my sister.

SARA

Oh.

CALLIE

They live in L.A. now. It's perfect.

SARA

Well at least, I don't mean to be crass but—

CALLIE

Yes, no, well I...like the apartment.

SARA

It's as big as mine and I'm sharing it with two other people.

CALLIE

Are they—did you...move here with any of them?

SARA

No, they came with the apartment. They're a couple. It's kind of awkward but, he's sweet, she's sweet, they seem to have a—

CALLIE

—sweet?

SARA

—relationshipthey'refine.

> CALLIE
> *(Nods)*

It's awkward.

> SARA

Rents are so—everything is—

> CALLIE

It's impossible to live here.

Pause. Sara studies Callie.

> SARA

You love it.

> CALLIE

You know, Sara, I've actually been to St. Louis and it's a quaint, pretty city but—what's the point of that? Everyone's still got their cars all geared up with clubs and car alarms and computerized keys. And you have to drive all the way across town to get to the good cheap places to eat. And *drive*, I mean you're in a city and you have to *drive* to get around?

> SARA

Where did you grow up?

> CALLIE

Tiny town upstate.

> SARA

Industrial?

> CALLIE

Countrified suburb. Tractor display in the middle of the mall.

> SARA

Pretty, though?

> CALLIE

I can't connect with mountains, trees, the little animals—they snub me. You know how you can be with two other people and you're all having a great time.

Then the person sitting next to you says something in French and the two of them burst into laughter, best laugh anyone's had all night. And you're left out because you took Spanish in the seventh grade, not French. That's what nature does to me. Speaks French to the other people at the table.

Slight pause.

                    SARA
I hate jazz.

                    CALLIE
You do?

                    SARA
I don't usually say that out loud because then people think I don't have a soul or something but I don't like the way it sounds. I don't like saxophones.

                    CALLIE
My sister played the saxophone.

                    SARA
I'm sorry—

                    CALLIE
I hate my sister.

                    SARA
The one who—

                    CALLIE
Yeah.

                    SARA
I hate your sister too.

Callie gives up a surprised smile; Sara does too. They hold it just a beat longer than normal, then Sara looks away.

                    CALLIE
So, do your friends think you're crazy?

SARA

Pff. Forget it. And my *parents* and Peter?

CALLIE

Huh?

SARA

—my ex. I mean I've never lived away from them. Even when I was in college I came home every weekend.

CALLIE

Close family.

SARA

It's...a cult. It's embarrassing, I should've moved...I mean, you were what, eighteen?

CALLIE

Don't look at me. I was going to go to one of those colleges that advertise on matchbook covers. My guidance counselor filled out my application to NYU.

SARA

I had to interview five times to get this fellowship. By the fourth one I had a rabbit's foot, rosary beads, crystals, a tiger's tooth and a Polynesian *tiki* all in my purse—now that I got this fellowship I have every god to pay.

Callie hands Sara a magic 8-ball.

SARA

What should I ask it?

CALLIE

Something whose answer you won't take too seriously.

SARA
(Addressing the ball)
Was moving to New York a good idea?

She shakes the ball, then looks at it.

SARA

It's sort of in-between two of them.

CALLIE

That means yes.

Another shared smile. Sara stands up.

SARA

I should go, I'm taking up too much of your—

Callie looks at her watch.

CALLIE

I told some friends I would meet them, otherwise I wish—

SARA

You should've said—

CALLIE

No—no—

SARA

I didn't mean to keep—

CALLIE

What're you doing this weekend?

SARA

I don't know. Unpacking. But then I gotta do something New Yorky, don't I?

CALLIE

Do you want to come over and I'll take you around the neighborhood? Show you some fun places to go to and eat—

SARA

Yes!

CALLIE

And you can hang out here, spend some time with...is it Caesar?

Sara rushes to the pet carrier.

SARA

Caesar, forgive me. He hates being in this thing.

CALLIE

Let him out.

Sara does.

SARA

He may be a little shy at first, in a new place with a new person—

CALLIE

You could come and visit him. Just let me know. I hope you'll feel—

SARA

Thanks, Callie.

CALLIE

For nothing, for what.

SCENE 2

A hospital examination room. Callie is sitting on an exam table but-toning the top button of her shirt. Detective Cole stands in front of her.

DET. COLE

Was he coming on to you, trying to pick you up?

CALLIE

He was just saying stuff, guy stuff, stupid kind of—

DET. COLE

What did you do?

She folds her arms protectively across her stomach like it was tender.

CALLIE

I—I wanted to leave—

DET. COLE

Your girlfriend?

CALLIE

My friend—Sara...said...something—

DET. COLE

What.

CALLIE

"Leave us alone" or something.

DET. COLE

And that's what set him off?

CALLIE

N—n—yeah. Well, she said—but then he said something
back and she told him...she said something—upset him.

DET. COLE

What'd she say?

CALLIE

...She sai—I think—

DET. COLE

What.

CALLIE

She told him to fuck off. Then he hit her.

DET. COLE

He hit her with his fist?

CALLIE

He hit her in her back then he grabbed her away—

DET. COLE

Grabbed her from you?

CALLIE

I—I was holding on to her arm with my hand like this—
(*She puts her hand on her other elbow*)
I wanted us to leave. But then he grabbed her and started banging her head against the building. And then he
smashed her head against his knee—like one of those
wrestlers—that's when she lost consciousness—and
then he smashed her again.

*Callie refolds her arms across her stomach. Detective Cole looks at
his report.*

DET. COLE

This was at Bleeker and West 11th—that little park.

CALLIE

Yes.

DET. COLE

At four fifteen in the morning?

CALLIE

Yes.

DET. COLE

What were you doing there?

Callie shakes her head.

CALLIE

...Just...walking around.

DET. COLE

Which bar were you at?

CALLIE

Excuse me?

DET. COLE

Four fifteen, honey, that's closing time.

CALLIE

Well we had been...we were at the White Horse Tavern.

DET. COLE

The White Horse. On Hudson Street.

CALLIE

Yes.

DET. COLE

Was there a good crowd there?

CALLIE

...Yeah? Pretty crowded.

DET. COLE

Did anyone at the White Horse try to pick you up, buy you or your friend a drink?

CALLIE

No.

DET. COLE

Did you talk to anyone?

CALLIE

Just to each other mostly.

DET. COLE

What did the bartender look like?

CALLIE

Excuse me?

DET. COLE

Bartender.

CALLIE

...It was a man.

DET. COLE

Short, stocky guy? Salt and pepper hair?

CALLIE

No.

DET. COLE

Kind of tall, skinny guy with a receding hair line? I know a couple of guys there.

CALLIE

I didn't really get a good look at him—Sara ordered the drinks. But I think he was tall.

DET. COLE

I'll go talk to him. Could be someone followed you from the bar. Maybe there was someone suspicious acting that you didn't notice. Bartender mighta seen something you didn't or talked to someone. What'd the bad guy look like?

CALLIE

He was tall.

DET. COLE

Like the bartender.

CALLIE

He was big—sort of, like he worked out.

DET. COLE

Was he black?

Callie shakes her head no.

DET. COLE

Hispanic?

CALLIE

It was dark, I couldn't—

DET. COLE

Short hair, long hair—

CALLIE

Short. Wavy, dark brown.

DET. COLE

You remember what he was wearing?

CALLIE

He had a leather jacket...jeans...some kind of boots. He was twentysomething, maybe mid.

DET. COLE

Like a college kid? Frat boy?

CALLIE

No.

DET. COLE

Like a punk?

CALLIE

No.

DET. COLE

Like what then?

CALLIE

...I don't know.

DET. COLE

Any markings on the jacket? A name or symbol?

CALLIE

No.

DET. COLE

So he sees a couple of good-looking girls walking—were you drunk?

CALLIE

Not at all.

DET. COLE

—he gives 'em a line, one of the women tells him to fuck off and he beats her into a coma. Anything else you want to tell me?

CALLIE

That's—that's what I...remember.

DET. COLE

Doctor done with you?

CALLIE

I think.

DET. COLE

Allright, I need you to go somewhere with me right now and look at some pictures.

CALLIE

Can you bring them here?

DET. C O L E

I need to take you there.

CALLIE

Because, my friend—if my friend...

DET. COLE

They say she's out of the woods in terms of life or—

CALLIE

But if she wakes up—

SCENE 3

Callie's apartment. Callie hangs up her jacket and Sara's. Sara sits on the junk-free couch.

SARA

I mean that's the way I am with the kids.

CALLIE

Sure, with kids it's o.k.

SARA

Why just them? Listen, every day when I walk by this park this guy, he's all cracked out, says something to me, you know, something nasty and I just lower my head and walk by.

CALLIE

Yep.

SARA

But yesterday, one of my students, Malik, is waiting for me outside the school and says he wants to walk me to the subway. So I say "sure" thinking maybe he has a problem he wants to tell me about. So we're walking and we pass by the park and I'm worried. "Is this crack-head gonna mention my vagina in front of this eight-year-old boy?" Sure enough, its "pussy this" and "booty that" and Malik says, "This is my teacher, watch your mouth." And the guy shuts up.

CALLIE

Still—

SARA

Freaking eight-year-old boy. I should be able to do that for myself.

CALLIE

The best thing to do is walk on by.

SARA

But it worked.

The phone rings. Sara looks up, but Callie doesn't.

CALLIE

Next time, just walk on by.

SARA

Why, what's ever happened to you?

CALLIE

Nothing and that's why.

The machine clicks on.

GEORGE'S VOICE ON MACHINE

Hey Callie, it's George. Your light is on, I know you're there. Jasmine and Lidia and I are at the Sinatra bar, where are you?

Callie walks toward the phone, then stops.

GEORGE'S VOICE ON MACHINE

Anyway, we'll be here for a while, so come hang out. Bye.

The machine clicks off.

SARA

I should go.

CALLIE

No no, they'll be there for hours.

SARA

I've taken up your whole—

CALLIE

Are you hungry? We could order in something. There's Polish, Indian, Cuban, there's a pretty good Vietnamese—

SARA

Are you sure you don't—I've never had Vietnamese—

CALLIE

I'll show you the menu.

Callie hops up and goes into the kitchen.

CALLIE

Something to drink? Beer?

SARA

Yes to beer.

Callie returns and hands her a bottle. Sara leans her head toward the phone.

SARA

Were those friends from work?

CALLIE

Oh no, the people at my job are a bunch of stiffs—can you imagine? They listen to the same news reports every 10 minutes for 8 hours a day. They repeat themselves even in regular conversations. No, George—the guy on the phone—Lidia, Jasmine...Rico, Sally, Ben— we were all friends in college and now we're stuck to each other. I think we're someone's science experiment, we just don't know it. A study in overdependency.

SARA

Is George your boyfriend?

Callie hands a menu to Sara.

CALLIE

I like the noodle dishes, they're on the back.

Sara takes the menu.

CALLIE

George and I...are friends. Who sleep together. But date other people. Sometimes for long periods of time.

We've been doing this since we were...twenty. Although he never likes anyone I'm dating, he's unabashedly—and I admit I can get jealous when he's—but at least I try to hide it, I'm pretty good at it too. It's only *after* they've broken up that I—Anyway, we'll probably get married.

Sara gets the 8-ball and shakes it. She looks up at Callie.

CALLIE

Or not.

SARA

It's stuck between two again.

CALLIE

Why's that keep happening to you?

SARA

Me? I think you have it rigged.

Callie takes the ball and shakes it. She looks at its answer (it's between two). Sara tries to look—

CALLIE

O.k., o.k.

SARA

All my friends are married or getting engaged, having babies or wishing they were—and lately when I hear about it, I think—why?

CALLIE

Why not?

SARA

Marriage. Why would you say to anyone, "I will stay with you even if I outgrow you."

Pause.

CALLIE
(Remembering)

Peter.

Sara is unresponsive, then finally nods.

CALLIE

Did you leave him to come here?

SARA

...No.

CALLIE

Mm...C-.

SARA

In what.

CALLIE

Acting.

Sara looks down.

CALLIE

I'm sorry—

SARA

No no—

CALLIE

I'm prying—

SARA

No, that's not why—

CALLIE

I hope I didn't—

SARA

No, it's o.k.

CALLIE

Did you decide what you wanted to order?

SARA

I moved out from our apartment—we lived together—and moved in with my parents about a month ago. I came here from there.

CALLIE

How—how long—

SARA

Seven years.

CALLIE

Seven...so you must still be—

SARA

—Finally. Finally where I want to be. I'll stay in New York for two years and then I'm going to take off.

CALLIE

Let me guess: India.

SARA

A for effort, but no. Australia, Malaysia, Indonesia, Micronesia—

CALLIE

All the countries that sound like skin rashes?

SARA

Peter said, "What about Anesthesia?" Mm. Speaking— what time is it?

CALLIE

Almost six.

SARA

Hm.

CALLIE

What?

SARA

Oh, he left a message on my machine saying he was going to call at six. He wants to come visit. He manages a restaurant in St. Louis so he wants to come and check out some of the special places here.

CALLIE

You'd better hurry.

SARA

I couldn't make it in fifteen minutes.

CALLIE

You could if you took a cab.

Slight pause.

SARA

But then I wouldn't have Vietnamese food.

CALLIE

We could do it another time.

SARA

I just started this beer.

Pause.

CALLIE

You wouldn't want to waste a beer.

SARA

That's what I was thinking.

CALLIE

Cheers.

They tap glasses. There is a sudden loud and rhythmic clomping on the ceiling. Callie doesn't respond.

CALLIE

I always get this. It's not too spicy.

SARA

What is that?

CALLIE

Crispy squid in a little salt and—

SARA

No, what is *that*?

CALLIE

Huh? Oh. Every Thursday and Saturday at 6.

SARA

What.

CALLIE

I think he teaches horses how to riverdance.

SARA

Have you complained?

CALLIE

It happens at exactly the same time twice a week for an hour. I just make sure I'm out or doing something loud.

SARA

Let's go up there.

CALLIE

No, no—

SARA

Why not?

CALLIE

We gotta stay here and wait for the food.

SARA

We haven't ordered it yet.

CALLIE
(About the food)
Yeah so what do you want?

SARA

Chicken.

CALLIE

What kind of chicken?

SARA

You're chicken.

CALLIE

No I'm not, I'm smart.

SARA

Allright, I'll go.

CALLIE

Sara. Come on, don't. Please.

Slight pause.

SARA

O.k.

CALLIE

I'm gonna order. What do you want?

SARA

Come on, let's go!

Police station house. Mrs. Winsley sits behind a table that Detective Cole is sitting on. She's wearing a sharply tailored business suit.

MRS. WINSLEY
He called them pussy-eating dykes.

DET. COLE
Come on, why would he call them that?

MRS. WINSLEY
Two women in a West Village park at four in the morning?
What's the chance they're *not* dykes.

DET. COLE
You tell me. You live in the West Village.

SARA
My husband and I have lived there for eight years.

DET. COLE
Like the neighborhood?

MRS. WINSLEY
I sure do.

DET. COLE
Lot of clubs and bars there.

MRS. WINSLEY
They even have ones for straight people.

DET. COLE
Is that why you live there?

MRS. WINSLEY

My husband and I have a beautiful apartment, Detective Cole. In a safe building on an otherwise quiet street. The fact that it's Graceland for gay people doesn't matter to me.

DET. COLE

So what were these girls doing?

MRS. WINSLEY

I didn't see—

DET. COLE

Were they making out, rubbing up against each other?

MRS. WINSLEY

I didn't see anything till I heard the other one screaming. I went to the window then I called nine-one-one.

DET. COLE

What'd you see then?

MRS. WINSLEY

He was beating on the both of them. I yelled down that I called the cops and I threw a couple flower pots at him. My spider plants—

DET. COLE

So the screams woke you up?

MRS. WINSLEY

I was in bed but up. Reading.

DET. COLE

Four thirty in the morning?

MRS. WINSLEY

I'm a fitful sleeper.

DET. COLE

You ever take anything?

43

MRS. WINSLEY

No.

DET. COLE

So you weren't groggy or half asleep?

MRS. WINSLEY

No.

DET. COLE

And you're sure you heard him call them dykes.

MRS. WINSLEY

I'm sure.

DET. COLE

And your husband?

No response.

DET. COLE

Your husband?

MRS. WINSLEY

He missed all the excitement.

DET. COLE

What'd he—sleep right through it?

Mrs. Winsley avoids his eyes.

DET. COLE

Oh...he wasn't home. Four thirty in the—is he a doctor?

MRS. WINSLEY

No.

DET. COLE

...Investment banker?

MRS. WINSLEY

Ha!

DET. COLE

Fire chief?

MRS. WINSLEY
He's a book editor, Detective Cole.

DET. COLE
I didn't know book editors worked so late.

MRS. WINSLEY
They don't.

DET. COLE
Was he...out having drinks with some buddies?

MRS. WINSLEY
He was obviously out, wasn't he.

DET. COLE
So you were waiting up for him.

MRS. WINSLEY
I'm a fitful sleeper, Detective. Have been since before I married him and those two girls are lucky that I am and that I was up and that I did something.

DET. COLE
You called nine-one-one.

MRS. WINSLEY
And my flower pots.

DET. COLE
Did you hit him?

MRS. WINSLEY
They fell near him. He stopped and took off.

DET. COLE
You stopped him.

MRS. WINSLEY
Well it wasn't the cops, took thirty minutes for someone to show up. You'd think it was Harlem, not the West Village.

SCENE 5

Callie's apartment. Callie walks on wearing jeans and carrying a fresh bouquet of flowers. She places them in a vase.

She goes into her bedroom and re-enters with several hangers of clothes. She looks at herself in the mirror as she holds up a tight blouse in front of her—too slutty—then drops it onto the floor. She picks up a shirt and holds it in front of her—too butch—then drops it onto the floor. She tries on a short skirt which she can't get past her hips. She throws the skirt onto the ground. She puts her jeans back on and puts on a third top—it looks like something Sara would wear.

The front door buzzer buzzes. Callie buzzes without asking who it is. She fusses over the flowers and accidentally knocks the whole thing over.

She gets the disobedient skirt and uses it to wipe up the mess. There is a knock on the door. Before Callie can open it, George walks in and stops in the puddle.

GEORGE
Hey Cal, when did they paint the—whoops!

Callie is stunned to see George but plays it off like it's about the puddle.

CALLIE
George!

George looks down.

GEORGE
Did you get a puppy?

CALLIE
Yeah, right.

Callie stands up.

GEORGE
So you're allright, huh?

CALLIE

Yeah, what?

GEORGE

No, I haven't heard from you in a while.

CALLIE

I'm fine, I'm fine...busy.

Callie goes to the kitchen to throw away the skirt.

GEORGE

Lidia said she called you about that book you were looking for, you didn't call her back.

CALLIE

...I forgot.

GEORGE

She got that job, you know.

CALLIE

No, I didn't!

George stretches himself out on the couch, stacking a pile of pillows behind his head.

GEORGE

Yeah, she's really excited.

Callie looks disapprovingly at his move.

GEORGE

We're gonna take her out on Friday night so try not to be "fine but busy" that night, o.k.?

He grabs the remote and clicks the t.v. on.

CALLIE

I'll remember. Um, George—

He looks at his watch.

GEORGE

I know, I know, we can watch your show. I just want to check to see what the score is.

CALLIE

I have plans for tonight.

GEORGE

Oh yeah, what?

CALLIE

I'm meeting someone for dinner.

George turns off the t.v. and sits up.

GEORGE

You have a date?

CALLIE

No!

GEORGE

With *who?*

CALLIE

It's not a date, I'm just meeting my friend Sara for dinner.

GEORGE

Who the hell is Sara?

CALLIE

I told you, that friend of a friend of a—
                    (*Refreshing his memory*)
She's new in town, I'm taking care of her cat—

GEORGE

I thought you said she was a big loser.

CALLIE

I said I didn't know, but now I do—she's not.

GEORGE

So what is she?

CALLIE

What.

GEORGE

What's she do?

CALLIE

She teaches up in the Bronx.

GEORGE

Oh, so she's a nut.

CALLIE

There's something wrong with us.

GEORGE

Why?

CALLIE

Because that's what I thought when she told me.

GEORGE

You have to wonder about people who want to do stuff like that. What does she want to do—save a life? Give a kid a chance? Or just feel good about trying.

CALLIE

She won a fellowship. She *competed* to get this job.

GEORGE

To teach in the Bronx? What'd the losers get?

The front door buzzer buzzes. Callie buzzes back.

GEORGE

You don't ask who it is anymore?

CALLIE

It's her.

GEORGE

You thought it was her when you buzzed me in.

CALLIE

You're right, that was a mistake.

Sara knocks at the door. Callie holds George's jacket open for him.

CALLIE

O.k. Please leave now.

GEORGE

Why?

CALLIE

Because I gotta go.

He stands up.

GEORGE

I'll walk out with you.

CALLIE

But I'm not leaving yet.

GEORGE

Huh?

Callie growls at George, then unlocks the door. Sara walks in.

CALLIE

Hey.

SARA

Hi, here, these are...

Sara shyly hands Callie a small bouquet of baby roses. Callie takes them.

CALLIE

Thank you. They're so—

SARA

They're—babies.

Callie goes to kiss Sara on the cheek, but retreats. Sara takes the cue late, now her head is sticking out. Callies tries to respond, but Sara has already reeled in like a turtle. Callie turns away, takes the other flowers out of the vase and puts the roses in.

CALLIE

I was just going to throw these out.

She crosses to the kitchen.

SARA

Hey, did you see they're filming a movie or something on the next block? Do you think we could stop on our way to the restaurant and watch for a while?

George steps out.

GEORGE

It's "NYPDBlue"—

Sara starts. She hadn't noticed him.

GEORGE

Oop—didn't mean to scare you.

SARA

No no, you didn't.

He crosses to her and extends his hand.

GEORGE

I'm George.

Sara shakes his hand.

SARA

Oh, *George*, I heard so much about you!

GEORGE
(Can't say the same thing)

...Nice to meet you.

Callie comes out of the kitchen.

CALLIE

Oh, sorry. Sara, this is George. George, this is—

GEORGE

We did this.

CALLIE

Good.
(To Sara)

We should go.

GEORGE
Where're you guys having dinner?

CALLIE
(Tries to slip it past him)
Vong.

George looks at Callie.

GEORGE
Dressed like that?

CALLIE
I didn't have time—

SARA
(Consoling)
You look great.

GEORGE
Well, tell me what you get.

SARA
Have you ever been?

GEORGE
Out of my league.

SARA
(To Callie)
Is it expensive? I don't want you to—

CALLIE
It's not expensive.

GEORGE
(To Callie)
You're treating? Then I wanna—

CALLIE
(To George)
You still owe me for my birthday.

SARA

Let's go dutch, Callie.

CALLIE

It's *my* treat.

GEORGE

What's the occasion?

Silence. There is none.

SARA

Actually, we're celebrating the fact that today LaChandra, one of my students, wrote her name for the very first time.

Callie looks down at her clothes.

CALLIE

I'm changing.

She runs off.

GEORGE

That's right, you're a teacher.

SARA

Mm hm.

GEORGE

Kindergarten?

SARA

Third grade.

GEORGE

And this kid wrote her name for the first time?

SARA

Perfectly.

GEORGE

Isn't that—

SARA

Wonderful?

GEORGE

...Yeah, isn't it?

Callie re-enters wearing the blouse she started off wearing.

CALLIE
(To Sara)
We should go, our reservation's at 8:00.

SARA

Do we have time to stop by? The NYPD—

CALLIE

Sure.

Sara starts for the door.

GEORGE

O.k., well um, bye. Nice to meet you.

SARA

Don't you want to come with us and watch them filming?

George flashes Callie a furtive look.

GEORGE

Mmm, I think I'll wait until it's on t.v.

He looks at Callie, she ushers him out the door.

CALLIE

Meanie.

GEORGE

Never take *me* to Vong.

Callie closes the door and locks it.

Scene 6

Police station house. Callie sits in an interview room. Detective Cole enters.

DET. COLE

Hey, thanks for coming in. You want some coffee?

CALLIE

Thank you, I'm fine.

He flips through his report.

DET. COLE

We were talking about the White Horse Tavern last time, right? On Hudson Street?

CALLIE

Yes.

DET. COLE

That's a famous bar, you know? Has a long literary tradition. They say Dylan Thomas died waiting for a drink there.

CALLIE

...I hadn't heard.

DET. COLE

I talked to the bartender there. I told you I wanted to ask him if he noticed anyone suspicious there that night. Maybe someone paying attention to you and your friend that you didn't notice.

CALLIE

Yes, you said.

DET. COLE

I went in and talked to Stacy, she said she don't remember you and your friend coming in.

CALLIE

It was pretty crowded.

Slight pause.

DET. COLE

Do you remember telling me that the bartender at the White Horse Tavern that night was a tall *guy*?

CALLIE

Sara ordered the drinks.

DET. COLE

So you didn't get a good look at the bartender.

CALLIE

I didn't.

DET. COLE

Not even enough to tell if it was a girl or a guy.

CALLIE

I'm sorry.

DET. COLE

So after you leave the White Horse, you and your friend go for a walk. You end up in that park area outside the playground. And you're...doing what?

CALLIE

We were sitting on one of the benches, talking to each other...when this guy says something.

DET. COLE

What'd he say?

CALLIE

Something like, "Hey, you want to party—"

DET. COLE

What did you say?

CALLIE

I didn't.

DET. COLE

Sara said something.

CALLIE

Yes.

DET. COLE

So she provoked him.

CALLIE

What!?

DET. COLE

She told him to "fuck off," and that's when he hit her, right?

CALLIE

No.

DET. COLE

I mean, if the two of you had ignored him or walked away, this wouldn't have happened, would it?

CALLIE

If *he* hadn't started—

DET. COLE

But Sara had to say something and that's what got him pissed, that's why he wanted to hit her. Why did she say something?

CALLIE

He started it, he—

DET. COLE

Allright. *He* must have said something first—something that upset her. What upset her so much?

CALLIE

He was bothering—

DET. COLE

What did he say? She said "Leave us alone," and then he said what?

Callie doesn't respond.

DET. COLE

Did he call her something?

CALLIE

What?

DET. COLE

Did he call her something. Like a name?

CALLIE

No.

DET. COLE

What's a name that might upset her?

CALLIE

I don't know.

DET. COLE

How about bitch?

CALLIE

No.

DET. COLE

He didn't call her a bitch?

CALLIE

I don't—

DET. COLE

A pussy-eating bitch?

Callie looks at Detective Cole.

CALLIE

No.

DET. COLE

What'd he say, then—

CALLIE

He shouldn't've—

DET. COLE

What'd he call her?

CALLIE

He called—

DET. COLE

What?

CALLIE

A fucking—

DET. COLE

Say it!

CALLIE

Fucking dyke! Pussy-eating dykes—both of us.

DET. COLE

Why would he say that, why would he call you that? Two
nice girls sitting on a park bench talking, why would he
call you dykes.

Pause.

CALLIE

Because we were kissing.

Detective Cole gestures—there it is.

CALLIE

It was the first—
We didn't know he was there. Until he said something.
"Hey, save some of that for me." Sara told him to leave

us alone. I couldn't believe she—then he offered to pay us. He said he'd give us 50 bucks if we went to a motel with him and let him watch. He said we could dry hump or whatever we like to do—turns him on just to see it. I grabbed her arm and started walking away. He came after us, called us fucking dykes—pussy-eating dykes. Sara told him to fuck off. I couldn't believe—he came up and punched her in the back, then grabbed her and pulled her away. I yelled for someone to call the police. He pushed her against the building and started banging her head against the building. He told her to watch her cunt-licking mouth. But he had his hand over her jaw, she couldn't—she just made these mangled—she was trying to breathe. I came up behind him and grabbed his hair—he turned around and punched me in the stomach. I threw up, it got on him. Sara tried to get away but he grabbed her and started banging her head against his knee. I tried to hold his arms back but he was stronger— he knocked her out. He pushed me to the ground and started kicking me. Someone yelled something—"Cops are coming"—and he took off in the opposite direction. West. He was limping. He hurt his knee.

(She looks at Detective. Cole)

That's what happened.

Callie's apartment. Sara is sprawled out on the couch holding several giant playing cards in her hand. She places a card on the discard pile and drains a glass of wine.

Callie brings a bottle of red wine from the kitchen; an empty one stands on the table.

SARA

O.k. If you're in someone else's bathroom and they have the toilet paper coming out from the bottom instead of the top—

CALLIE

I hate that.

SARA

Do you change it or leave it the way it is.

CALLIE

What do you mean change it? You'd change somebody else's toilet roll?

SARA

If I was gonna use it a couple times.

CALLIE

Pfff.

SARA

Allright, you go next.

CALLIE

So if you were driving down a highway and saw a pothole in the road ahead what would you do, straddle or swerve?

SARA

Mm, straddle. You?

CALLIE

Straddle.

SARA
(*About Callie*)

Swerve.

CALLIE

Nah ah.

SARA

Yes you would.

CALLIE
(*A second scenario*)

Cat in the road.

SARA

Caesar!—say a rabbit.

CALLIE

O.k., a rabbit. Straddle, swerve or brake.

SARA
(*Like this is an option*)

Straddle a rabbit.

CALLIE

Sport utility vehicle—four-wheel drive, you could.

Callie sits down, picks up her cards and discards.

SARA

Screech to a brake, check the rabbit, then—smoke. You?

CALLIE

Brake.

SARA

Swerve.

CALLIE

Why do you keep saying that?

SARA

This is you—

She grips her hands around an imaginary steering wheel. She fills her eyes with panic, turns the wheel a hard right, then a fast left.

Callie puts her cards down.

CALLIE

These cards are driving me nuts.

SARA

One more hand, please.

Callie picks the cards back up.

CALLIE

Can I ask you something about your job?

SARA

Yep.

CALLIE

Why did you want it?

SARA

You mean this fellowship?

CALLIE

Public school, the Bronx—teaching.

SARA

Instead of private school, St. Louis—teaching?

CALLIE

That's what you're used to, right?

SARA

It's where I *worked* for five years, I never got used to it. I mean, I never went to private school. We all went to the cruddy public school—I mean, it was cruddy compared to the private school, it's the Sorbonne compared to where I teach now. But in a private school...I mean, what am I giving them? They have more than everything.

CALLIE

And the Bronx?

SARA

These kids—you know who I was when I was their age? I was the kid who had the right answer, knew I had the right answer but would never raise my hand. Hoping the teacher would call on me anyway. Those are my favorite kids to teach. And here? Now? I got a classroom full of them.

Callie looks at the discard pile.

CALLIE

Did you pick up a card? You have to pick a card.

Sara does.

SARA

You should come and meet them one day.

CALLIE

Yeah, o.k.

SARA

I'll bet you've never even been to the Bronx.

CALLIE

I go everyday.

SARA

Fly over.

CALLIE

That's more than most New Yorkers.

SARA

Can I ask you about your job?

CALLIE
(*Dread-filled*)

Go ahead.

SARA

Why the traffic?

CALLIE

Why the traffic indeed.

SARA

I mean, as opposed to news reporting or other kinds of journalism.

CALLIE

I'm not a journalist. I never worked in radio or t.v. before I got that job.

SARA

So how'd you get it?

CALLIE

My boyfriend Tom's uncle worked at the station.

SARA

Oh.

CALLIE

I mean, it's the traffic it's not even—*the weather.* You just ride around in a helicopter and tell people what the cars are doing.

SARA

The helicopter part is pretty great, right?

CALLIE

Yeah, how great?

SARA

Well if you don't like it you should get another job.

CALLIE

I can't.

Sara imitates Callie swerving in her imaginary car again.

CALLIE

I don't get that.

SARA

What time is it?

Callie looks at her watch.

CALLIE

Two thirty.

SARA

Already? Is the subway o.k. this time of night?

CALLIE

You should take a cab.

SARA

How much will that be?

CALLIE

About ten bucks?

SARA

I'll take the train.

CALLIE

I'll give you the money—

SARA

I have it, it's just too much. It's only 4 or 5 stops on the train.

Callie sits up a little.

CALLIE

Listen you can...you know, you're welcome to stay...this pulls out to be a sofa bed...you can take a train in the

morning, when it's safe. I'm not getting up for anything
in particular.

SARA

Maybe Caesar will come sleep with me.

CALLIE

Yes! You can reconcile with your cat!

SARA

He's holding such a grudge. He never comes out when
I'm here.

CALLIE

It took a few days before he started to sleep with me.

SARA

Lucky.

Slight pause.

CALLIE

I'm sure he'll sleep with you tonight.

SARA

Yeah.

CALLIE

Here, let me just get those—

*She pulls off the cushions; Sara helps. Together they pull out
the bed.*

CALLIE

I think it's comfortable, I haven't slept on it myself—
because I live here—but if it's not comfortable enough
then I'll switch beds with you. In fact, should we just do
that? You sleep in my room and I'll sleep out here?

SARA

No, no, this'll be fine.

CALLIE

I think it's comfortable.

Callie bounces on it once, then gets up.

CALLIE

Is there anything else you need?

SARA

I think I'm all set.

CALLIE

Allright. Sleep tight.

SARA

Goodnight.

They stand there. Finally, Callie smiles and walks off into her room. Sara takes off her shirt just as Callie re-enters with a tee-shirt.

CALLIE

Do you need a tee—whoop.

Callie looks away.

SARA

Oh—I have one.
        (*She pulls one out of her bag*)
We did face painting today so I—

CALLIE

I'm sorry.

Sara puts the shirt on. Callie leaves.

SARA

Its o.k.

CALLIE
(*Offstage*)

Goodnight.

SARA

Sweet dreams.

Sara gets in bed and shuts out the light. She lies there a minute. Then,

SARA

Psss pssss psss psss psss.

She lifts her head up and looks for Caesar.

SARA

Caeeeesar.

No sign of him. Sara lies there another minute.

SARA

Come on you grudge holder. Pssss psss psss.

Nothing. Finally,

SARA
(To Callie in the other room)
Is he in there with you?

CALLIE

Uh uh. He's not out there with you?

SARA

No.

Callie walks up to her doorway.

CALLIE

Is he under your bed?

Sara leans over and looks.

SARA

No.

Callie shrugs at Sara.

SARA

Will you do me a favor? For just like a minute?

CALLIE

Sure.

SARA

Would you just lay in bed here for just a minute to see
if he comes.

CALLIE

O.k.

SARA

Since he's been sleeping with you.

Callie gets in next to Sara and pulls the covers up.

CALLIE

I guess we have to convince him we're sleeping.

SARA

Oh, right.

They lie down.

CALLIE

This bed is comfortable.

SARA

Isn't it?

CALLIE

I never laid on it before.

SARA

It's comfortable.

CALLIE

I got it second-hand.

SARA

Really?

CALLIE

A hundred and fifty bucks.

SARA

That's cheap.

CALLIE

It's comfortable.

Pause.

SARA

Are your feet hot?

CALLIE

What?

SARA

My feet get hot when I sleep.

CALLIE

Even in winter?

SARA

Yeah.

CALLIE

Take them out.

SARA

I usually move the sheet so that it goes the other way,
you know, the short way—

CALLIE

O.k.

*Sara gets up and turns the sheet around so that both pairs of their
feet are exposed. She lies back down.*

Pause.

SARA

Do you see him?

CALLIE

Who?

71

SARA

Caesar.

CALLIE

Not yet.

They both lie there staring at the ceiling. After a while,

CALLIE

Huh?

(Pause)

Are you asleep?

No response. Callie turns and looks at Sara.

CALLIE

You're not asleep already, are you?

No response. Callie draws her feet under the covers and turns her back to Sara. Sara opens her eyes.

SCENE 8

Callie's apartment. There's loud banging on her door. Callie enters from her bedroom, wearing pajamas. She looks through the peephole.

CALLIE

Allright George, I hear you!

She unlocks the door and opens it. George bursts in wearing his bartender uniform.

GEORGE

How long have you been home?

CALLIE

Lower your voice.

GEORGE

Why didn't you answer your phone?

CALLIE

I don't know.

GEORGE

You wanna know how fucked up and worried about you everyone is right now?

CALLIE

No.

GEORGE

You wanna know how I heard?

CALLIE

No.

GEORGE

You wanna know exactly what drink I was making at the moment I heard your name on the goddamn t.v.?

CALLIE

No, I don't.

GEORGE

Dirty martini. T.V.'s on in the background. I hear about this gay bashing, two women attacked, and I sort of pay attention, not really. I'm making this drink and thinking about how I gotta run downstairs and get some more peanuts. And then I feel my ears close and my face gets all hot, like I just swallowed a mouthful of hot peppers. So I turn to the t.v., but now they're talking about some apartment fire. So I switch the channel and they're just starting the story. Gay bashing. Woman in a coma. Callie Pax.

CALLIE

I'm not in a coma.

GEORGE

What?

CALLIE

Sara's in a coma.

GEORGE

How do I know that?

CALLIE

What was I—

GEORGE

How do I know anything but what I see on the goddamn—

CALLIE

What did you want—me to call you from the hospital?

GEORGE

Yes!

CALLIE

What would I say? On a pay phone. In the hospital. Sara lying in a room swollen and blue, face cracked open, knocked out, not responding to anything but the barest reflex—all because...because—

GEORGE

Come and get me. That's what you could've said.

Pause.

GEORGE

Are you hurt?

Callie doesn't respond.

GEORGE

Did a doctor look at you?

CALLIE

Sara's hurt.

GEORGE

Nothing happened to you?

Callie doesn't respond. He walks toward her; she walks away.

GEORGE

Callie—

CALLIE

Bruises.

GEORGE

Where.

CALLIE

Cracked rib.

GEORGE

Let me see.

CALLIE

It's nothing.

GEORGE

Let me see.

CALLIE

There's nothing to see.

Pause.

GEORGE

Do you want me to call anyone?

CALLIE

No.

Slight pause.

GEORGE

Do you want me to spend the night?

CALLIE

No.

GEORGE

Do you want me to go?

Slight pause.

CALLIE

No.

Pause.

CALLIE

George, do you remember the first time we kissed?

GEORGE
(Thinks about it)

No.

CALLIE

Me either.

Pause.

CALLIE

You know, I would stand here at the door with Sara and say "goodnight," "take care," "see ya tomorrow," "get home safe—"

When what I *really* wanted to do was plant her a big, fat, wet one. Square on the lips. Nothing confusing about it. She wouldn't have to think "Maybe Callie meant to kiss me on the cheek and...missed." You know, just right there. Not between friends. Not a friendly kiss at all. Bigger. So she'd know. She'd know for sure. That I was answering her. Sara is always asking me, "What do you *want, Callie?*" And finally, I let her know. I answered.

Scene 9

Callie's apartment. Callie walks in from the kitchen carrying a roasting pan in two mittened hands. She pulls the top off and rears her head back as the smell assaults her. She reaches in and pulls out a drumstick; it's fossilized. She bonks it on the table, it sounds like a baseball bat.

There's a knock on the door—Callie starts. She looks out the peephole and sees Sara. She hurries to hide the roasting pan and all signs of cooking.

She opens the door, and Sara steps in.

> SARA
> The kids talked about you the rest of the day, you were hilarious.

> CALLIE
> *(Shady)*
> How'd you get in?

> SARA
> Huh? Oh, there was this woman with a baby carriage. I held the door for her, then squeezed in behind her. It smells like something in here.

> CALLIE
> Like what?

> SARA
> Like someone vomited in sawdust. Oh—I brought you this—
> *(She hands her a bottle of wine)*
> For coming in and talking to the kids.

Callie silently takes it and sets it down.

CALLIE

It's a little early for me.

SARA

It's...almost six.

CALLIE

Go ahead, you have some.

SARA

Don't open it for me.

CALLIE

O.k.

SARA
(Trying to figure her out)
So, what'd you do the rest of the day?

CALLIE

Nothing.

SARA

Nothing?

CALLIE

Nothing.

SARA

You know Michelle, the girl who had the sweater with the puppet on it today? She used to say "nothing" just like that. Until I squeezed an answer out of her.

CALLIE

Those kids adore you.

SARA

Do you think?

CALLIE

You have a knack for them.

SARA
(As if it's the first time she's heard it)
Thank you.

CALLIE
It was humiliating for me.

SARA
Why?

CALLIE
Standing up there talking about my idiotic job.

SARA
You ride in a helicopter, Callie, what could be cooler than that?

CALLIE
Have you noticed? The only thing you ever praise about my job is that I ride in a helicopter?

Pause.

CALLIE
But that doesn't even matter. Standing up in front of those kids today telling them about what I do I thought—why should these kids care about traffic, their families don't have cars. I don't have a car. No one I care about has a car. Who am I helping?

SARA
(Gently)
People with cars.

CALLIE
Who are they? Why do they live in New York City? Why have a car when you hear every 10 minutes on the radio that the traffic is so bad?

SARA
Maybe you should look for another job.

CALLIE

Whose uncle's gonna get it for me this time?

SARA

You could get a job based on your experience.

CALLIE

As a traffic reporter?

SARA

What do you want to do instead?

CALLIE

I don't know.

SARA

Allright. Come on, we can think about this. What do you like?

CALLIE

I don't want to do this.

SARA

You know a lot about food...you have great taste in restaurants—

CALLIE

I don't—I really don't want to do this.

SARA

You should become a chef!

The noise from upstairs starts again. Callie goes for her coat.

CALLIE

Let's get the hell out of here.

SARA

You could go to cooking school—

CALLIE

Let's see what's playing at the three-dollar movie theatre.

SARA

You obviously have some kind of talent for food—

CALLIE

Come on, put your coat on, let's go.

SARA

God, what is that smell?

CALLIE

I think someone downstairs was trying to cook something.

SARA

Ugh, you think that smell is related to food?

Callie opens the door for Sara.

CALLIE

Barely.

They exit.

SCENE 10

Sara's hospital room. Callie walks in and stands at the foot of Sara's bed. What can she do? She thinks a beat. She remembers.

She untucks the sheet and rolls it back so that Sara's feet are exposed. She tucks the sides of the sheet in so that it'll stay that way.

Scene 11

Callie's apartment. Callie, dressed up, is impatiently waiting for Sara. She refuses to sit—she paces across the apartment, picking up things, scowling at them, then putting them down.

Finally, there's a buzz. She buzzes back and puts on her coat. Sara knocks, and Callie opens the door—Sara is holding a wet newspaper over her head.

> SARA
> Wow, it's really starting to come down now.

> CALLIE
> That means it's gonna be hard to get a cab.

Sara looks at her watch.

> SARA
> We still have time.

> CALLIE
> Not really.

> SARA
> We can be a little late, can't we?

> CALLIE
> Sara, I asked you to be here by 5:30.

> SARA
> I know, I'm sorry, I lost track of time.

Sara takes off her coat.

> SARA
> Let me just stand next to the radiator for a second.

CALLIE

Is that what you're wearing?

SARA

...Yeah.
                    (She looks at her clothes)
What?

CALLIE

Nothing.

SARA

I mean, is this a dress-up event?

Callie shrugs.

SARA

What are you wearing?

CALLIE

Just...clothes.

SARA

Let me see.

CALLIE

It's just...what I wore to my hippie friend's wedding.

SARA

Let me see?

Callie opens her coat a little bit.

SARA
(Embarrased)

Oh, you look great.

Callie shuts her coat.

SARA

I'm underdressed.

CALLIE

We don't have time to stop by your place.

SARA
Can I borrow something of yours?

CALLIE
Let's just forget it, I don't want to go.

Callie sits with her coat on.

SARA
I thought you had to.

CALLIE
Technically.

SARA
Isn't your station getting an award?

CALLIE
They are, I'm not.

SARA
So do you want to go or not?

CALLIE
I have to.

SARA
O.k., let's go.

Sara makes for the door. Callie remains seated.

SARA
What's going on.

CALLIE
Nothing.

Pause.

SARA
Why are you still sitting down?

Callie shrugs.

SARA

Let me see what you've got in your closet.

Sara goes to her bedroom and comes back holding a dress on a hanger.

SARA

Could I wear this?

CALLIE

I wore that to a reception last week.

SARA

You did, I didn't.

CALLIE

People will recognize it.

SARA

Do you care?

Callie shrugs.

SARA

Callie, what the hell.

CALLIE

I don't know.

SARA

O.k. Just tell me. What do you want?

CALLIE

I have to go to this thing.

SARA

Do you not want me to go? Is that it?

CALLIE

You don't have to go if you don't want to.

SARA

Callie, will you say what you want?

CALLIE

I have to go, I have to.

SARA

So let's go.

CALLIE

What are you going to wear?

SARA

What?

Callie gets up.

CALLIE

I have to go to this thing and I want you to go with me but I don't want you to wear what you're wearing and I don't want you to wear my clothes. What will people think if we walk in together and you're wearing my clothes?

Sara sits down.

SARA

I'm not going.

CALLIE

Now this.

SARA

I'm tired, I'm underdressed, I'm not going to know anyone there except for you—forget it.

CALLIE

Sara, I asked you to go to this thing with me a week ago; I told you it was an awards ceremony, why did you dress like you were going camping?

SARA

You didn't make it sound like it was that big a deal.

CALLIE

An *awards ceremony?*

SARA

If you had wanted me to get dressed up, you should've told me.

CALLIE

I told you to be here at 5:30, you couldn't manage that.

SARA

What's the big deal—you don't even like your job.

CALLIE

I don't like my job the way you love your job but that doesn't mean you shouldn't come at the time I asked you to, wearing something appropriate.

SARA

Obviously this is more important than you—

The clomping from upstairs starts again.

CALLIE

There's my cue. I'm leaving now, I don't care what you do.

SARA

Yeah go, get chased out of your own apartment again.

CALLIE

What?

SARA

Better to plan your life around someone else's schedule than have to face them and tell them what you have every right—

CALLIE

What do you care? What do you care? This is my apartment—

SARA

You're pathetic, Callie—

Callie takes off her coat.

CALLIE

Fuck it, I'll stay right here then.

SARA

Perfect.

CALLIE

You can leave.

SARA

Glad to.

CALLIE

I'm busy tomorrow so forget about the museum.

SARA

Yeah, I'm busy too.

Callie opens the door for Sara. Sara grabs her coat and exits. Callie slams the door behind her.

Scene 12

Hospital waiting room. Peter is aready sitting; Callie walks in; Peter looks up and forces a smaile, as he would to any stranger. Then it hits him. After a beat—

CALLIE

Her parents?

PETER

Anita and Joe are in there now, yeah.

Silence.

CALLIE

They're strict about that—the hospital. Two at a time.

PETER

Noah's ark.

CALLIE

Excuse me?

PETER

Two at a—
    (He shakes his head at himself)
—stupid.

More silence.

CALLIE

Did you—was your flight o.k.?

PETER

There were like six peanuts in the whole—
    (He covers his eyes)
Flight was fine, fine. Thank you.

CALLIE

Her parents, are they—how are they?

PETER

Anita is...wrecked, *and* Joe—they're...I mean, Sara's their only daughter—

CALLIE

I know.

PETER

They never wanted her to come here—

CALLIE

I know.

PETER

The doctor said she can't be moved until she regains consciousness.

CALLIE

They want to move her?

PETER

Mm hm.

CALLIE

Back to St. Louis?

PETER

To Chesterfield, where Anita and Joe live. It's about twenty minutes outside.

Pause.

CALLIE

But what—what if she doesn't want to go?

PETER

Why wouldn't she?

CALLIE

Because the fellowship, she wanted—she worked so
hard to get, and the kids—

PETER

Her old school would take her back in a heartbeat.

CALLIE

Her old school, but she—

PETER

But—I mean we have no idea when she'll be able to
go back to work—or *if*. The doctors can't say. There
could be permanent...she'll need rehabilitation, maybe
home care—

CALLIE

I know.

PETER

She needs her family. And they need to take care of her.

Silence.

PETER

...There was a response.

CALLIE

Excuse me?

PETER

The doctor. He said Sara responded to—he told her to
squeeze his hand and she...squeezed.

CALLIE

She did?

PETER

Yeah.

CALLIE

She did!

PETER

Fucking A.

CALLIE

Amazing!

PETER

I thought you'd want to know.

Callie looks him in the eye.

CALLIE

Thank you.

(pause)

Sara...Sara told me...nice things...about you—so many...

Pause.

PETER

She didn't tell me about you.

Callie looks down.

PETER

She said you were a friend.

Pause.

CALLIE

I am her friend.

Pause.

PETER

And that you knew good restaurants to go to—

He looks at Callie.

PETER

That's all Sara told me about you.

CALLIE

I see.

PETER

Sara and I—

CALLIE

She told me.

Pause.

PETER

We lived together for—

CALLIE

Yes.

Pause.

PETER

I still—

CALLIE

Yes.

Pause.

PETER

I'd like—I'd like you to tell me what happened that
night.

*Silence. Peter waits long enough to figure out Callie's not going to
answer.*

PETER

Please.

Slight pause.

CALLIE

I'm sorry.

PETER

What.

CALLIE

I can't.

PETER

Why can't you?

Slight pause.

CALLIE

Everything you need to know has been in the papers, on the t.v.—

PETER

I've seen the newspapers and the t.v.

CALLIE

Then you know every—

PETER

No, I don't know everything. I know what *time* it happened, I know *where*, and I know that you were there. And now you're here and *Sara* is in there. That's the part I want to know about. Why is *she* in there?

CALLIE

I wish it was me but it isn't.

PETER

Why isn't it?

Callie doesn't respond.

PETER

Were *you hurt?*

CALLIE

You don't know what fucking happened.

PETER

Tell me!

Callie doesn't answer.

PETER

Why couldn't you protect her?

CALLIE

He was big, he was stronger—I tried—

PETER

How big?

CALLIE

I *tried.*

PETER

Bigger than me?

Callie turns away from him.

PETER

Could I have—

He turns her back.

PETER

Hey, was he bigger than me?

CALLIE

No!

Peter steps back.

PETER

Why was she protecting you?

Callie holds on his eyes but doesn't answer.

Scene 13

Callie's apartment. The phone rings. Her machine picks up. Callie runs in from the bedroom and picks it up.

CALLIE

Hello?

Dial tone sounds over the speaker. She hangs up. She hovers over the phone for a moment. She jerks the receiver up to her ear, dials three numbers then abruptly hangs up. She stares at the phone.

She picks up the phone, dials seven numbers then hangs up.

She picks up the phone and places it on the floor in front of the sofa.

CALLIE

Caesar, please? Come on, you've known her longer than I have. I'll dial her number for you. Tell her I—tell her I thought about—just tell her to come over.

Caesar doesn't come out.

CALLIE

If you were a dog you'd do it.

Callie picks up the phone and dials seven numbers quickly.

CALLIE

Hi George, it's me—what. Did you just call here—why not? Yeah, Vong was great. I got the sea bass with cardamom, Sara got the grilled lamb chops with coriander—yeah she eats meat, why wouldn't she? I don't know what you're talking about—Listen, what are you doing for dinner? 'Cause I just walked by Tomoe and noticed there's no line. Come on, I need a sushi fix. Allright, if you get there first just tell them—I know you know. O.k. bye.

Callie hangs up. She puts the phone back on the floor.

CALLIE

O.k. Caesar, second chance.

Scene 14

Sara's hospital room. Callie walks in and stands at her bedside.

CALLIE

They're finished building that building across from your apartment.

Sara doesn't respond.

CALLIE
(Conversation volume)

Wake up now.

No response.

CALLIE
(A little stronger)

Sara.

No response.

CALLIE

Can you hear me?

Callie looks down. Nothing.

CALLIE

Open your eyes.

No response.

CALLIE

Open your eyes.

No response.

CALLIE

They're gonna start you on physical therapy tomorrow. Just little stuff, range of motion, something to get your blood moving.

Pause.

CALLIE

You've gotten all these cards and letters, I'll read some to you later.

Pause.

CALLIE

You know your parents are here. They're doing their best—I think they're doing o.k., considering. You getting better makes them feel better—yeah.

Pause.

CALLIE

They look at me...your parents look at me...like I'm some dirty old man.

She waits for a response.

CALLIE

And the newspapers, the t.v, the radio—my station, my own station, when they ran the news about the attack, they identified me—"Traffic reporter for this station." Now everybody—the guy at the deli—I used to be the blueberry muffin lady, now I'm the lesbian traffic reporter whose lover got beat up. And I've gotten letters—from two women, their girlfriends were *killed* during attacks—and they wrote me these heartbreaking letters telling me what they've been through...and they tell me to speak truth to power and I don't know what that *means*, Sara. Do you?

Do you know me?

Callie leans in closer.

CALLIE

Do you know who I am?

Sara opens her eyes.

CALLIE

Oh my God. Hi.

SCENE 15

Callie's apartment. Callie walks in from the bedroom in her bare feet, wearing a t-shirt and underwear. She pours two glasses of water and drinks from one. George enters from the bedroom wearing jeans and pulling on a t-shirt. Callie hands him the second glass of water. He takes a sip.

GEORGE

Deer Park?

CALLIE

You can't tell.

GEORGE

Tastes like plastic.

CALLIE

You want Evian, you buy it.

GEORGE

Not Evian, *Vermont Natural Springs.*

CALLIE

It's Deer Park or Dos Equis, George. That's what I've got.

GEORGE

Dos Equis, please.

Callie hands him a beer.

GEORGE

You got any snacks?

CALLIE

I think I have some wasabi peas.

GEORGE

Those *green*—

CALLIE

Taste like sushi—

GEORGE

Oh *shit.*

CALLIE

What.

GEORGE

I have to go.

CALLIE

Where?

He goes to get the rest of his clothes.

GEORGE

It's someone's birthday at work so a bunch of people are going out to that Japanese tapas place on Ninth Street afterwards, I promised I'd meet them.

CALLIE

Blow them off.

GEORGE

I can't.

CALLIE

Come on. We'll go to Aggie's in the morning for breakfast. Banana pancakes.

GEORGE

I'm sorry, Callie. I made these plans before you called.

CALLIE

Whose birthday?

GEORGE

This new girl at work. I don't think you've met her.

CALLIE

Let me guess. She's an actress.

He puts on his shoes.

GEORGE

She's classically trained.

CALLIE

You gotta get out of the restaurant business, George. Broaden your dating pool.

GEORGE

I'll call—I'll see you on Wednesday, at Jasmine's, right? She's having everyone over for dinner.

CALLIE

Yeah, I put it down.

He gives her a quick kiss on the lips.

GEORGE

Bye.

He exits, and Callie closes the door behind him. She pours his beer down the drain. There's a knock on the door.

CALLIE
(Calling)

I didn't lock it.

Sara opens the door halfway and takes a small step in.

SARA

I saw your light on—

Callie turns around, unconsciously pulling on the bottom of her t-shirt.

CALLIE

I—I'm not—I didn't know it was you.

SARA

I saw him—he didn't notice me.

CALLIE

Just...just give me a second.

Sara steps back into the halway as Callie pushes the door closed and goes to her bedroom. She comes back out wearing a sweater over her t-shirt and a pair of sweat pants.

She opens the door. Sara enters carrying a bottle of wine.

SARA

I think—I think you'll like this kind.

Callie takes it and gestures toward the couch. Sara steps tentatively in and sits down on the edge of it.

CALLIE

I'll get us some glasses.

Callie heads for the kitchen.

SARA

You don't have to open it now—it's late, I just wanted to—

Sara gets up and follows Callie.

SARA

Apologize, Callie. You've been so good to me since I came here. I'm embarrassed that I acted, that I said—

CALLIE

That I'm a loser?

SARA

I didn't—

CALLIE

That I'm pathetic.

SARA

You're not pathetic.

CALLIE

I do, I know—I sometimes...swerve. I was thinking...you know, when I was little, my parents made me take tennis lessons—I'm not an athlete—neither are my parents, I don't know why—because the lessons were free! And it was summer, and my parents didn't want me sitting around the house doing nothing, which is what they thought I was doing—which was...true. So, they made me take these lessons, even though I was a klutz. And I tried— but I was a natural klutz. Still, at the end of the summer we all had to play in these championships and compete against the kids from the other classes. So for the first round, I get pitted against this kid who obviously took tennis lessons because she wanted to be a really good tennis player. I can't even return her serves. The match takes like 10 minutes. Afterwards, my parents can barely speak, they feel so bad. They take me to Dairy Queen, tell me to order whatever I want—I get the triple banana split, and for the rest of the summer they let me sit around and watch Love Boat reruns, which is all I wanted to do anyway.

Callie hands Sara a glass of wine.

SARA

It was a good show.

CALLIE

But lately, I feel like...there's something...worth...winning.

SARA

Callie, I know that neither you nor I have ever—well at least I know that I haven't, I've never really asked—

CALLIE

By the way, I did get an award.

SARA

What?

CALLIE

An award for traffic reporting—who knew?

SARA

Are you serious?

CALLIE

I'm sorry, I interrupted—

SARA

Did you know?

CALLIE

What.

SARA

You knew you were going to get an award, didn't you?

CALLIE

I swear I didn't.

SARA

Is that why you were so—

CALLIE

Sara, I could never have known. Trust me.

SARA

Did they call you up to the dais and everything?

CALLIE

Just like the Oscars.

SARA

I wish I had seen.

Sara touches Callie's hand.

CALLIE

I wish you'da been there.

Callie squeezes Sara's hand. Slight pause.

CALLIE

You want to see it?

SARA

Yes!

Callie roots through a pile of papers .

CALLIE

I thought I stuck it in here.

Sara goes to the sofa and lifts the pillows.

SARA

(Sotto voce)

Sometimes I find stuff in here.

Sara pulls out a plaque and holds it in the air.

SARA

I found something.

CALLIE

There it is!

Sara looks at it. She walks over to the bookshelf and slides some pho-tographs out of the way.

SARA

Put it here, o.k.?

CALLIE

Not there.

SARA

Why not?

CALLIE

Everyone will see it.

SARA

Just keep it there.

Callie reaches for it.

SARA

Stop it.

Callie takes her hand away, but reaches for it again.

SARA

I mean it.

Callie takes her hand away. Sara takes the plaque, exhales on it, rubs it on her shirt, then puts it back.

SCENE 16

Sara's hospital room. A nurse is writing on her chart. Callie walks in.

CALLIE

Any good news?

NURSE

She's stable.

CALLIE

I guess that's good news.

NURSE

Her bruises are healing.

Callie looks at Sara's face.

CALLIE

Yes.

NURSE

Can tell she's a pretty girl.

CALLIE

Yeah.

NURSE

She's a schoolteacher?

CALLIE

She is.

NURSE

Where?

CALLIE

In the Bronx.
(*Makes eye contact with the nurse*)
Third grade. She has thirty-five kids. She knew all of
their names by the end of the first day.

NURSE

Takes a lot to be a public school teacher in New York
City.

CALLIE

She's got it.

NURSE

Those kids are lucky.

CALLIE

They know it.

NURSE

I'm gonna give her her bath now.

CALLIE

Oh, allright.

She starts to leave.

NURSE

I'll show you so you can do it.

Callie stops. Slight pause.

CALLIE

Oh—that's very—but I don't think I should, I've
never—

NURSE

You've seen the worst of her. Most of her bruises are on her
face. Her body looks fine. There's nothing to be afraid of.

CALLIE

I don't know if she'd want me to.

NURSE

It won't hurt my feelings, you know. I'm sure she'd like it better if you do it.

CALLIE

...Right now, though, I have to go.
                    (She taps on her watch face)
The time. But...thank you.

She heads out.

SCENE 17

Callie's apartment. Callie and Sara walk in. Sara carries groceries; Callie carries a bag from a record store.

CALLIE

Which airport is he flying into?

SARA

JFK.

CALLIE

At eleven in the morning.

SARA

Eleven-thirty.

CALLIE

Have the car service pick you up at around ten-thirty, tell them to take the BQE to the LIE to the Van Wyck—that'll get you to the airport by eleven. But tell the driver to take the Midtown Tunnel back; it'll cost you three-fifty but the Manhattan bound traffic on the Williamsburg Bridge will be too heavy.

SARA

Check.

Sara looks through the CDs.

SARA

Do you ever go out dancing?

CALLIE

Sometimes I do—my friend Sheila goes to this club on Wednesday nights, and sometimes she invites a bunch of us girls to go.

CALLIE

SARA

I'd like to go sometime.

CALLIE

...Sure...

SARA

Will you let me know next time you go?

CALLIE

A bunch of us girl friends go...it's fun...the music's great, and it's fun, you don't have to worry about guys trying to pick you up...'cause it's all women. I like to go there and dance, there's this kind of warm—like when you go to the bathroom, there's only one line and everyone's really nice and smiles...

SARA

Have you ever...asked someone to dance?

CALLIE

We kind of stick to each other—us friends. Sheila usually knows a bunch of women there, and I've met them.

SARA

You ever meet a woman there, that seemed...interesting...to you?

CALLIE

...No.

(pause)

Not there.

Pause.

CALLIE

Have you—?

SARA

What.

CALLIE

In St. Louis, do they—or have you been to?

SARA

We have a couple places like that but I've never been. My friend Janet says that only college girls go to the clubs and bars; older lesbians just stay home and read. That's what everyone in St. Louis does, stays home and brews their own beer or does their email.

Slight pause.

CALLIE

But I mean, have you ever...?

SARA

Of course, right? I mean, right? I mean I can't imagine any woman who's never *felt* attracted—

CALLIE

Right!

SARA

It's just, I mean if you've never—

CALLIE

You want a beer?

SARA

Love one.

CALLIE

I hope I have some.

SARA

What time is it?

CALLIE

Just about six.

SARA

Uh oh.

CALLIE

What?

SARA

I promised my roommates I'd clean the apartment by
the time they came back from their trip, and they're
gonna be home in an hour.

CALLIE

Just—wait here a couple more minutes.

SARA

I really should go.

CALLIE

Just wait one minute.

SARA

Why?

CALLIE

I wanna...show you something.

SARA

Callie—

CALLIE

Take my watch.

Callie takes off her watch and hands it to Sara.

CALLIE

What time is it now?

SARA

Five-fifty-nine.

CALLIE

And how many seconds?

SARA

Thirty-eight seconds.

CALLIE

And what day is today?

SARA

Thursday.

CALLIE

What time is it now?

SARA

Five-fifty-nine and fifty seconds.

CALLIE

So count 'em.

SARA

What?

CALLIE

Count 'em down. Five seconds, four—

SARA

Four, three, two, one—what.

Callie opens her hands toward Sara.

SARA

What?

Callie points toward the ceiling.

Callie gestures—I did it.

SARA

It's quiet. Oh! It's Thursday at six! And it's quiet!

*Sara opens her arms, and they hold each other. They keep holding.
Callie lets go.*

SARA

I'll call you tomorrow.

CALLIE

O.k.

Pause.

SARA

Um, see ya.

CALLIE

O.k. Bye.

Sara opens the door and lets herself out. Callie ambles slowly over to the sofa, looks at the door, buries her head in a pillow and screams.

Scene 18

A coffee shop. Mrs. Winsley is sitting at a table. Callie walks in.

CALLIE

Mrs. Winsley?

MRS. WINSLEY

Yes.

Callie extends her hand; Mrs. Winsley shakes it .

CALLIE

I'm sorry I'm late. I came straight—

MRS. WINSLEY

It's fine, it's fine. I don't have to meet my husband until eight.

Mrs. Winsley gestures for Callie to sit.

CALLIE

Please.

MRS. WINSLEY

Should we order something? Coffee or tea?

CALLIE

Coffee would be great.

MRS. WINSLEY

How are you doing?

CALLIE

I'm o.k.

MRS. WINSLEY

Yeah?

CALLIE

I want to thank you for...what you did, Mrs. Winsley.

MRS. WINSLEY

I only did what I should've.

CALLIE

Not everybody—

MRS. WINSLEY

How's your girlfriend?

CALLIE

Sara—she's better. Alert and responding. We just have to wait to see what kind of effect. How much and what.

MRS. WINSLEY

I read in the paper she's from Kansas or something.

CALLIE

St. Louis. Missouri. Kansas City is in Missouri, but Sara's from St. Louis.

MRS. WINSLEY

I'm from outside Cincinatti myself, although I've been here for twenty years. When I first moved here I would smile at strangers on the subway, give quarters to beggars on the street.

CALLIE

Sara gives a dollar.

MRS. WINSLEY

So I can imagine what it must've seemed like to her. Small-town girl in the big city—seeing men dressed as women, women holding hands—must've seemed like gay paradise to her.

Slight pause.

CALLIE

St. Louis is not a small town.

MRS. WINSLEY
What hospital is she at?

CALLIE
St. Vincent's.

MRS. WINSLEY
How are the doctors there? Are you pleased with them?

CALLIE
It's hard to say. You want them to do everything, you just want them to make her better. But they do what they can. I think they're o.k.

MRS. WINSLEY
I know they have limited visiting hours, but a situation like this, they must let you stay all day.

CALLIE
I have to go to my job—

MRS. WINSLEY
Of course. Of course you do.

CALLIE
But I do visit every day.

MRS. WINSLEY
It must be exhausting for you.

CALLIE
Well, her family's here—

MRS. WINSLEY
Are you close with them?

CALLIE
No...Not close.

MRS. WINSLEY
I know what it's like with in-laws. It took years before mine...Have you and Sara been together long?

CALLIE

Um...no.

MRS. WINSLEY

Oh, I'm sorry I thought you two were—

CALLIE

I know.

MRS. WINSLEY

Here I've been going on and on as if—

CALLIE

Yes, you were.

MRS. WINSLEY

So you're not really—

CALLIE

No, like I said I go there every—

MRS. WINSLEY

But you're not really involved.

Scene 19

Callie's apartment. George, wearing jeans and a dress shirt, checks himself out in the full-length mirror. Callie walks in from the bedroom wearing a dress.

GEORGE

I'm a little strapped 'cause business was slow last night.

CALLIE

Just don't worry about it.

GEORGE

I brought fifty bucks.

CALLIE

That'll get you a salad.

GEORGE

How expensive is this place?

CALLIE

Expensive.

GEORGE

Why do we have to go to a place like that? Why can't we just go to Benny's Burrito's and drink a bunch of margaritas.

CALLIE

I *told* you, I'm gonna pay for the whole thing so stop stressing out about it.

She pushes George out of the way with her hip and looks at herself in the mirror.

GEORGE

O.k. Miss Traffic Reporter of the Universe or whatever
you are, I'm gonna get the lobster.

CALLIE

They have venison.

GEORGE
(Even better)

Ooo!

Callie turns toward him.

CALLIE

Does this dress make me look fat?

GEORGE

I *can* not, *will* not, *ever* answer that question.

CALLIE

I'm changing.

She heads for the bedroom.

GEORGE

What are you so uptight about?

CALLIE
(Off stage)

I'm not uptight.

GEORGE

That's the third time you've changed. Who is this guy
anyway?

CALLIE
(Off stage)

Sara's ex.

GEORGE

Why do you need to look so good for him?

Callie comes back on wearing a different dress. She stands in front of the mirror.

CALLIE

It's a nice restaurant.

GEORGE

Is he gonna be dressed up? You told me I could wear jeans.

CALLIE

Because I knew you'd wear jeans anyway.

GEORGE
(Has to admit she's right)

Hm.

George stands next to Callie; he looks at their reflection. He puts his arm around her waist.

CALLIE

So how was the birthday party the other night?

She wriggles away.

GEORGE

Fine.

CALLIE

Did the birthday girl get everything she asked for?

GEORGE

You want to talk about this?

CALLIE

No.

GEORGE

Cool.

Pause.

CALLIE

Did you fuck her before or after midnight?

GEORGE

Nice.

CALLIE

I'm just wondering about the technicality—

GEORGE

Listen, I'm not like you and that guy—

CALLIE

Who?

GEORGE

Who was that, that guy with the nose ring that you—

CALLIE

Hey—

GEORGE

In the bathroom of the—

CALLIE

Hey—

GEORGE

With no protection.

The buzzer buzzes.

CALLIE

I told you *that?*

GEORGE

I asked.

CALLIE

We should start keeping more to ourselves.

GEORGE

Too late.

CALLIE

Don't say that.

GEORGE

Why not?

CALLIE

Makes me feel old.

GEORGE

We are old.

CALLIE

You are.

There's a knock on the door. Callie opens it. Sara walks in alone. Callie looks behind her.

CALLIE

...Hi.

GEORGE

Hey, how's it going.

SARA
(Small)

Hi.

CALLIE

Where's Peter?

SARA

He...uh, left. You look beautiful. You too, George.

CALLIE

He left...New York?

SARA

Yeah, he changed his flight. He left a couple hours ago. I told him to tell the driver to take the Van Wyck.

CALLIE

Something happen at work?

SARA

No it—I asked him to leave.

Callie moves closer to her.

CALLIE

Oh, um—
> *(She looks at George, then back at Sara)*
Listen, we don't have to go out—

GEORGE

Yeah, no, if you're upset—

SARA

No, it's fine, I want to go out. I want to get to know George.

CALLIE

Are you—did something happen—

Again she looks at George: Why can't he disappear?

CALLIE

I mean, you don't have to—

George stands behind Callie and puts his hands on her shoulders. She looks at his hands like they are dead frogs.

SARA

He was being so—he was criticizing everything. "Your apartment's too small. It's in a bad neighborhood. Your school is dangerous. It's too far away." All he could talk about was how dirty and dangerous everything is.

CALLIE

...Well—

GEORGE

It *is*.

SARA

What? Compared to St. Louis? I don't want to live there. I've started something here, and I—that's what— because it's...

I love...New York!

> GEORGE
> (Nods)

Mm.

> CALLIE

Let's go eat.

> GEORGE
> (To Sara)

Are you sure?

> SARA

Yeah.

> GEORGE

Great! Let's go!

George offers Sara his arm. She takes it. He offers his other arm to Callie.

> CALLIE

I'll catch up with you.

> GEORGE

O.k.
> (To Sara, on the way out)

They have venison you know.

> SARA

You mean Bambi?

George and Sara exit. Callie walks over to the magic 8-ball, shuts her eyes a moment, then wiggles the ball. She looks at its answer.

> CALLIE
> (Quietly)

Yes!

She puts down the ball and hurries to catch up with them.

SCENE 20

Sara's hospital room. She's sitting in a wheelchair, eyes open. Peter sits next to her reading from a book.

> PETER
>
> "And then ninety-eight kilometers—that's sixty-one miles—north of Wilcannia is a lunar landscape." That looks lunar, doesn't it? "Some of the locals don't mind showing off the interiors of their white-walled subterranean settlements"—You'll want to sign up early for *that* tour, gonna be a regular *Who* concert trying to—

He looks at Sara, clears his throat then goes back to the book.

> PETER
>
> As I was saying. "Looping around about one hundred and sixty kilometers"—that's a hundred miles to you and me—"a road leads to Mootwingee, a surprising patch of greenness in the barren Bynguano—" Australia *is* an English-speaking country, isn't it?

He fingers the last few chapters of the book.

> PETER
>
> You know, I'm dying to see how this ends but can we—

Sara nods. He kisses her hand.

> PETER
>
> Thank you. We'll save the big finish for after dinner.

He puts the book away and picks something up.

> PETER
>
> Did you see this?

He holds a homemade greeting card in front of her. Callie steps into the room, then steps back. She watches.

PETER

You got a card from your old class at Friends. See, there's Matthew and Sophia and Emily—your favorite, the anti-Christ. She writes, "I hope you feel bitter and come bark soon." I see your replacement is letting her spelling skills slip.

Sara tentatively takes the card in her hand.

PETER

Hey! Get you.

I've been talking to Jenny and Steve a lot, keeping them updated. Jenny's been letting everyone know what's going on. Margaret's called, Jamie, Lisa—it's frustrating for them not to be able to see you. They picture the worst, all they have are the images in their heads from reading the newspaper articles. It'll be better for them when they can see you.

The doctor says we can move you soon. Your parents and I have been talking. I agree that you should stay with them after you get out of rehab. You're welcome to stay at our old place, of course, if you want to, I would take off from work so that I could—well, I'm going to take off from work anyway.

Pause.

PETER

Just because you're coming back home I'm not going to act like everything is going to be the way it was. I know you went to New York because you wanted to change things.

He touches her face.

PETER

You do want to go home—

Water drops from Sara's eyes.

PETER

Don't you?

Callie turns, walks toward Sara's nurse, who is standing at her station.

CALLIE

Excuse me.

NURSE

You're back.

CALLIE

Do you have time now? To show me how to do it?

Scene 21

Callie's apartment. Callie and Sara enter after having left the restaurant. Callie takes off her coat, Sara doesn't.

CALLIE

Uugggh, I'm so full, it hurts to move. What do you want to do, we could watch a movie if you—

SARA

Let's uh...let's go out, let's go somewhere.

CALLIE

Where do you want to go?

SARA

There's a bar. In the West Village. Henrietta's, you ever been?

CALLIE

Once.

SARA

Will you go with me?

CALLIE
(She looks at her dress)

Like this?

SARA

We could change. Friday night, it's supposed to be a good night.

CALLIE

O.k.
(Slight pause)
Good for what?

> SARA

There's supposed to be a lot of people there.

> CALLIE
> *(Nods, though she doesn't quite understand)*

O.k., let's go.

> SARA

You change, and then we can stop by my place, and then we'll go.

> CALLIE

We don't—you can borrow some of my clothes.

> SARA

Really? That's great. That's *great*.

They stand there.

> SARA

You go ahead and change and I'll...change next. I'll wear whatever's left over.

> CALLIE

I'll go change.

> SARA

Maybe we'll like it there—

She looks helplessly at Callie.

> CALLIE
> *(Trying to be helpful)*

Yeah, o.k.

> SARA

Let's just—

> CALLIE

We'll go, we'll hang out, have a drink.

SARA

Yes! You know, maybe meet people.

CALLIE

Are you—I mean, do you...want to *meet* people?

SARA

Yes!—No! I want to meet people to—meet people maybe make friends but no, I don't want to meet *someone*, some stranger—

CALLIE

We'll just go.

SARA

It's just a bar.

CALLIE

With a whole bunch of lesbians in it.

SARA

And us.

They lock eyes, hoping the other will say something perfect.

They keep waiting.

Scene 22

The hospital. Sara's sitting in a wheelchair. Callie enters carrying a bag.

CALLIE

Sara.

Sara turns to her.

CALLIE

I brought you stuff to change into.

She pulls some clothes out of the bag.

CALLIE

Don't you think?

Callie puts them in Sara's lap.

CALLIE

We're gonna do this. Watch me. You gotta listen to me too.

She undoes Sara's gown.

CALLIE

O.k., we're gonna start with the left side because we're taking things off.

She takes off Sara's left sleeve.

CALLIE

And now the right.

She helps Sara pull her arm out of the right sleeve. She takes out a bra.

> CALLIE

This closes in front. Can you...go like this?

She lifts her arms at the elbows. Sara does it.

> CALLIE

Good for you. I should tell—

She looks around for the nurse.

> CALLIE

Later.

She puts the bra on.

> CALLIE

So far so good.

She takes the shirt off Sara's lap.

> CALLIE

Nice shirt, huh? Did I pick out a nice shirt for you? O.k., you're gonna need to sit up a little for me.

Sara sits up. Callie puts the right sleeve on.

> CALLIE

If I can just—am I hurting you? I'm sorry, Sara—I'm sorry—

> *(To herself)*

Relax.

She puts the left sleeve on.

> CALLIE

This one you can do. Push—push—keep breathing, and push—

Sara pushes her arm through the sleeve.

> CALLIE

It's a girl!

Callie buttons Sara's shirt.

CALLIE

Let's keep you warm. It's cold in this place.

Callie takes the pants. She helps Sara's right foot off the foot rest.

CALLIE

We're gonna do this together. I'll do this one.
(*She points to her left*)
That one you can do.

Sara lifts her left leg off; it spasms.

CALLIE

Oh—oh. O.k. O.k.

Callie flips the foot pads up. She scrunches up the right leg of the pants and wrangles it on.

CALLIE

We gotta work together on this one, o.k.?

She scrunches up the left leg. Sara lifts her leg.

CALLIE

Are you helping me? Yes. You are.

Callie takes out a pair of shoes.

Now, the shoes go last. Like this.

Callie puts her right shoe on.

CALLIE

And like that.

Sara slips her left foot in the left shoe.

Callie pushes Sara's feet closer to her. Callie stands up.

CALLIE

Now you're gonna stand up. I'm gonna help. One, two, three—

She puts her hands under Sara's arms and lifts her up. She pulls her pants up. They sit back down down.

                              CALLIE

    I can do this, you see?

Sara nods.

                              CALLIE

    Choose me.

Sara smiles.

Scene 23

Sara and Callie are walking down the street, having just left Henrietta's. Finally, Sara turns to Callie.

SARA

What—was I thinking.

CALLIE

That was like—going to a birthday party when you don't know the person whose birthday it is.

SARA

I don't know why I was expecting...I don't know what I was expecting. What time is it?

Callie checks her watch.

CALLIE

Around four.

SARA

So late.

CALLIE

Should we...go somewhere—where do you want to go?

SARA

I don't know—

CALLIE

Let's just...keep walking.

SARA

Sure.

They walk a few steps in silence. After a while,

CALLIE

How do you eat corn on the cob. Around the world or typewriter style?

SARA

Typewriter.

CALLIE

Me too.

SARA

What kind of person eats around the world?

CALLIE

I don't know.

SARA

I mean, what is that based on? You read left to right, right?

CALLIE

I do.

SARA

So you should eat your corn that way too.

CALLIE

Do you think in Egypt they eat right to left?

SARA

I don't know.

CALLIE

Fascinating question, though.

SARA

Do you wait *in* line or *on* line?

CALLIE

Oh. Now I wait on line. But I used to wait in.

SARA

But physically, you're *in* a line, not *on* one, right?

CALLIE

Yeah, stick by your guns. I caved in.

SARA

You say on. I say in.

CALLIE

What about this?

Callie plants her one. They pull away.

SARA

Huh.

CALLIE

What?

SARA

You just did that.

CALLIE

Yes I did.

SARA

Nice.

They come at each other, but with their heads angled toward the same side. They bump noses.

CALLIE

Whoop—

SARA

Sorry—

They back away. Callie puts her arms around Sara's waist and pulls her toward her.

SARA

Do you think we should—

CALLIE

I don't want to go anywhere, I don't want to change anything. Let's just—

SARA

O.k.

CALLIE

Try again.

They get their heads right, connect lips, put their arms around each other.

And kiss.